Angelina Ballerina™

Center Stage

Based on the stories by Katharine Holabird
Based on the illustrations by Helen Craig

SIMON SPOTLIGHT
An imprint of Simon and Schuster Children's Publishing Division
New York London Toronto Sydney New Delhi
1230 Avenue of the Americas, New York, New York 10020 • This Simon Spotlight paperback edition December 2019 • Illustrations by David Leonard

For information about special discounts for bulk purchases, please contact Simon & Schuster Special Sales
at 1-866-506-1949 or business@simonandschuster.com • Manufactured in the United States of America 0521 LAK
3 4 5 6 7 8 9 10 • ISBN 978-1-5344-5482-8 • ISBN 978-1-5344-5483-5 (eBook)

The town of Chipping Cheddar was bustling with excitement. The spring festival was just around the corner, and Miss Lilly's Ballet School had been rehearsing for their annual performance of *Mouse Lake* for several weeks.

Angelina Ballerina was the most excited of all. She had been chosen to dance the lead role of Mouse Princess. It was her dream come true!

Every day Angelina skipped and twirled happily all the way to ballet rehearsal.

Then, one day when Angelina arrived, everyone looked upset. "Angelina!" cried her best friend, Alice. "Miss Lilly sprained her ankle! How will the show go on?"

Angelina gasped. What were they going to do?

Miss Lilly arrived, limping into the studio and clutching Miss Quaver for support.

"I'm afraid I cannot choreograph the rest of the ballet," Miss Lilly told the class. "Angelina, could you direct the dancers for me this time?"

"Me?" Angelina asked nervously. "I don't know if I can . . ."
"We believe in you, Angelina!" cheered Alice.
"Please, Angelina?" asked the rest of the dancers.

Angelina didn't like to give up the role of the Mouse Princess, but she knew she couldn't let down Miss Lilly and the dancers.

"Of course I will help," she said.

Just then, Angelina had an idea. She whispered it to Miss Lilly, who smiled and nodded.

"Alice," Angelina called. "Will you dance the role of the Mouse Princess?"

"But you've worked so hard for this role," Alice began, "and I don't think I dance as well as you!"

"I know you can do it!" Angelina said encouragingly.

Alice agreed to dance the lead role, while Angelina would choreograph the routines. The best friends gave each other a hug.

All of the dancers got into position.

"Plié, then kick!" called Angelina.

The dancers all followed her instructions and worked hard together. Angelina smiled. She was having just as much fun choreographing as she did when she was dancing!

Alice was a little nervous at first, but she kept trying her best. By the end of the day, Alice could do an arabesque just like Angelina!

The rest of the week, everyone pitched in to help prepare for the show. Alice and the other dancers kept practicing their routine.

Henry painted the sets.

Flora and Felicity helped assemble the costumes.

And Angelina kept directing.

Finally, it was the day of the performance!
Angelina and Alice were nervous.
"What if I make a mistake?" Alice asked Angelina.
"What if I let everyone down?" Angelina asked Alice.

Just then, Miss Lilly arrived. "Don't worry, my little mouselings. No matter what happens, remember that working hard and doing your best are the most important things of all," she told them.

The music started. Angelina gave Alice a hug. "You can do it," she whispered.

Alice smiled and leaped out onto the stage. She didn't forget a single step, and she loved dancing as the Mouse Princess.

When the performance was over, Miss Lilly presented Alice and Angelina with two red roses.

"Brava," she cried, "to the cast of *Mouse Lake*; our lead dancer, Alice; and our choreographer, Angelina Ballerina!"